DANIEL TIGER'S NEIGHBORHOOD

Daniel Goes Out for Dinner

adapted by Maggie Testa

based on the screenplay "A Night Out at the Restaurant"

written by Becky Friedman

poses and layouts by Jason Fruchter

Ready-to-Read

Simon Spotlight

New York   London   Toronto   Sydney   New Delhi

SIMON SPOTLIGHT
An imprint of Simon & Schuster Children's Publishing Division
1230 Avenue of the Americas, New York, New York 10020
This Simon Spotlight edition September 2020
For information about special discounts for bulk purchases, please contact Simon & Schuster Special Sales at
1-866-506-1949 or business@simonandschuster.com.
Manufactured in the United States of America 0522 LAK
10
ISBN 978-1-4814-2873-6 (eBook)
ISBN 978-1-5344-7337-9 (prop)

Hi, neighbor!

We are going out for dinner.

What food do you think looks yummy?

I want the

chicken and broccoli.

Yum!

We tell our waiter what we want to eat.

Our waiter will bring the food to the table.

Now we have to wait for our food to be cooked.

It is very, very
hard to wait.

My mom knows
what we can do.

"When you wait,
you can play, sing,
or imagine anything."

But what can we do
at the table?

"You can play a quiet, sit-down game," says my dad.

"We can play 'what is missing,'" says Katerina.

Look at the things
on the table.

Katerina hides

one of the things.

What is missing?

The salt was missing!

That was fun.
The food is
still not here.

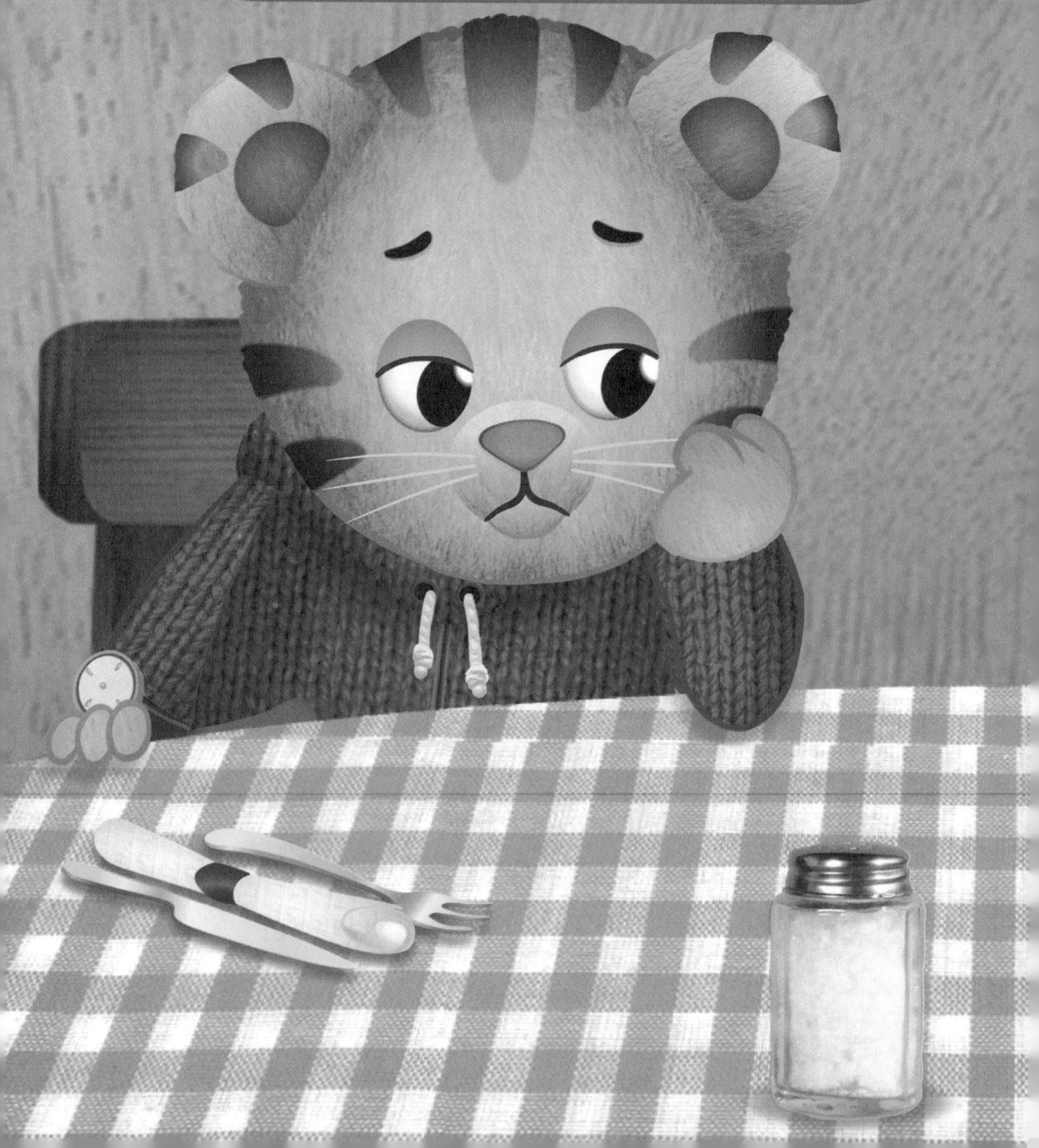

We still have to wait.

What should we do
while we wait?

When you wait,
you can play, sing,
or imagine anything.

We can imagine that the things on the table can play with us!

We do not have to wait anymore.

The food is here.

It is time to eat!

I am glad I waited
for my food.

It is so yummy!

I can play, sing,
or imagine anything
to make waiting easier.